Making Memories
Entertaining Family & Friends

Marissa Castellano

Making Memories
Entertaining Family & Friends

Marissa Castellano

First Edition

ISBN-10: 1-933177-38-1
ISBN-13: 978-1-933177-38-0

Library of Congress Control Number: 2011937110

Published by
M Creations, LLC
P.O. Box 192694
Dallas, TX 75219

Production by
Lone Star Productions
13820 Methuen Green
Dallas, TX 75240

Photographs by
Colleen Kelly
Bob Manzano
Rob Frehse
Mark Davis

Graphic Design by
Biz Haddock
Zibbydot Dezigns
www.zibbydotdezigns.com

Printed in Canada

IMPORTANT: Recipes with alcohol in them are not intended for children. Follow appropriate authorities' guidelines for safe temperature, washing, and preparing of food. The advice, ideas and recipes contained herein may not be suitable for your situation. You should consult with a professional where appropriate. Neither the publishing company nor author shall be liable.

TABLE OF CONTENTS

INTRODUCTION

Over the years, through occasions ranging from big family holiday parties, to intimate evenings with friends, I have come to take great pleasure in entertaining. Now I am excited to share my tips and tricks for holiday and party entertaining with you!

Growing up in an Italian family, we had many wonderful holiday gatherings. My whole family would get together and everything was planned perfectly—from the delicious food to the pretty table décor. That is where I learned the pleasure of entertaining.

In creating this book, I have drawn information and inspiration from these occasions, from family and friends who have generously shared their recipes, from cooking/entertaining literature, and from my own experimenting– in the kitchen and dining room, as well as the living room and patio!

Included in this book are, of course, recipes... but also, *entertaining holiday traditions, decorating ideas, music and activities to complete your celebration.* This book is a convenient reference for holiday and sports parties.

I am happy to share my favorite ideas so others can enjoy them as well. The best part about holidays and parties is the time together with those we love—this is when we make our most treasured memories.

Enjoy, have fun, and make some memories....

Marissa Castellano

CHECKLIST & COUNTDOWN

Checklist for every party...
The items listed below are important to keep in mind for every holiday/ party in the book.

Candles
Plates
Bowls
Serving Utensils
Silverware
Ice
Pitchers
Cups
Napkins
Tablecloth or Runner
Flowers

Countdown for every party...

At least two weeks before: send out invitations.

One week before: make sure you have all the items on the checklist.

Two days before: grocery shopping and flowers.

One day before: set table, set up decorations, and get as much cooking and/or prep work done as possible.

The day of party: finish food preparation as early as possible; try to leave an hour before guests arrive for you to relax.

Let the parties begin...

NEW YEAR'S DAY

Start the year off right with great food and lots of fun!

- Décor: Red/White/Black colored decorations
- Theme: Board games
- Table: Place board game pieces in a glass vase
- Activities: Play your favorite games
- Music: Karaoke
- Favors: Little candy gift boxes of red and black candies

Creating the Menu

Sparkling Water

V-8 Juice

Cheese & Crackers

Chicken Soup

Hearts of Palm Salad

Popovers with Strawberry Butter

Red, White & Black Candies

Cookies

CHICKEN SOUP
Serves 8

Ingredients

6 cups water
5 pound chicken
2 tablespoons salt
1 ½ pounds baby carrots
1 medium size onion, cut in half
4 celery sticks, diced
3 plum tomatoes

In a large pot, add 6 cups of water. Bring water to a boil. Wash and clean chicken and place in the pot (breast-side down). Add salt, baby carrots, onion, and celery. Place the three tomatoes in a small bowl and squish with a fork. Add the tomatoes to the large pot. Cook for an hour over medium-low heat. Remove onion before serving.

POPOVERS WITH STRAWBERRY BUTTER
Serves 8

POPOVERS

Ingredients

2 large eggs
¾ cup milk
¼ cup water
1 tablespoon unsalted melted butter
¾ cup all purpose flour
½ teaspoon salt

Preheat oven to 375 degrees F. Generously grease 9 (½ cup) muffin tins. In a bowl, whisk together eggs, milk, and water and add butter while whisking. Add flour and salt. Whisk mixture until combined well but slightly lumpy. Divide batter among muffin tins and bake in lower part of oven for 45 minutes. Cut a slit on top of each popover with a small sharp knife and return to oven for 10 minutes.

STRAWBERRY BUTTER

Ingredients

1 pound unsalted butter, softened
1 cup strawberry preserves

Mix the butter until light and fluffy. Add the preserves and mix until well combined.

HEARTS OF PALM SALAD
Serves 7

Ingredients

2 heads Boston lettuce
1 cup pine nuts
1 can hearts of palm
20 cherry tomatoes
1 can kalamata olives
 Citrus Herb Vinaigrette

Wash lettuce and dry. Add hearts of palm, cherry tomatoes, kalamata olives, and pine nuts. Mix all together. Pour on desired amount of Citrus Herb Vinaigrette dressing. I use Citrus Herb Vinaigrette by a company called Seeds of Change.

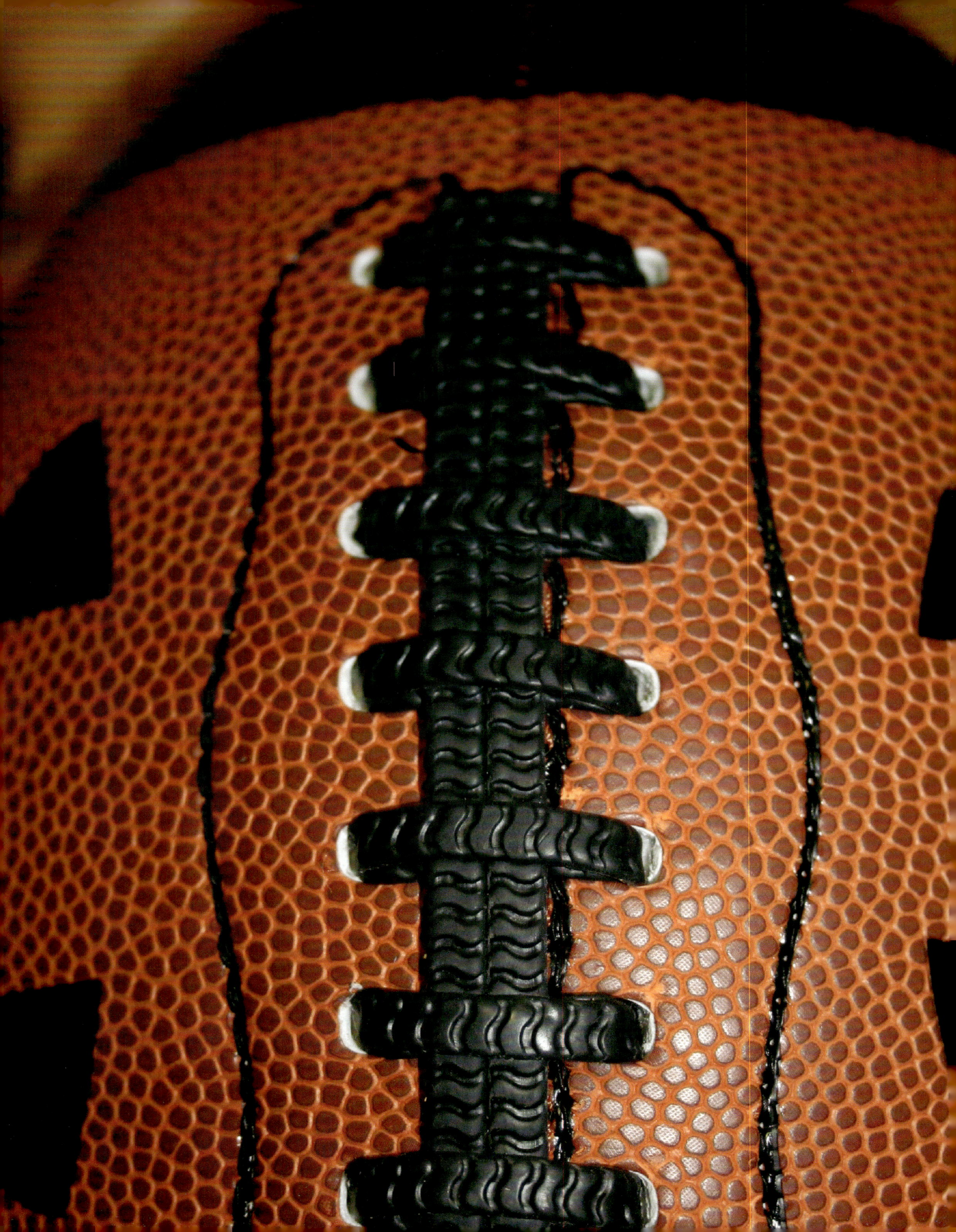

COLLEGE BOWL GAMES

Let's go....

- Décor: Big Screen TV
- Table: Choose team colors, use football decorations from a party store, make it buffet style, put decorations down the center of the table
- Activities: Choose various outcomes during the game for prizes
- Favors: Take home leftover cupcakes

Creating the Menu

Beer

Root Beer

Chips & Salsa, Nuts

Artichoke Dip

Sausage Sliders with Spinach & Peppers

Beef Enchiladas

Chocolate Cupcakes with Peanut Butter Filling

ARTICHOKE DIP
Serves 8

Ingredients

2 cans artichoke hearts, finely
  chopped
1 cup mayonnaise
½ cup Parmesan cheese
½ teaspoon garlic salt

Preheat oven to 350 degrees F.
Combine the artichoke hearts,
mayonnaise, Parmesan, and garlic salt
in a bowl. Then transfer mixture to a
baking dish. Bake 20 to 30 minutes (or
until golden).

SAUSAGE SLIDERS WITH SPINACH & PEPPERS
Serves 8-10

Ingredients

2 tablespoons olive oil
2 large onions, thinly sliced
2 red bell peppers thinly sliced
2 bunches spinach (8 cups), stems
   removed
2 pounds sweet Italian sausage
24 small rolls split
½ teaspoon salt
⅛ teaspoon black pepper

Preheat broiler. On stovetop, heat olive oil in a large skillet over medium heat. Add onion, salt and pepper, stirring occasionally until the onion begins to soften, 5 to 6 minutes. Add the bell pepper and cook, stirring occasionally, until softened, 5 to 6 minutes. Add the spinach and cook, tossing, until the spinach is just wilted, 1 to 2 minutes.

Meanwhile, remove the sausages from their casings and shape into twelve ½ inch thick patties. Place them on a broiler proof rimmed baking sheet and broil until cooked through, 4 to 5 minutes per side. Make sandwiches with the rolls, sausage patties, and vegetable mixture.

BEEF ENCHILADAS
Serves 8

Ingredients

1 box yellow rice
1 pound lean ground beef
1 tablespoon olive oil
1/4 cup onion, chopped
1 can refried pinto beans
1 tablespoon pre-packaged taco
  seasoning or to taste
1 can (16 ounce) salsa
8 tortillas
1 package shredded Mexican
  cheese

Prepare yellow rice according to recipe on box.

Preheat oven to 350 degrees F. Heat olive oil in a large pot. Put 1 pound of ground beef in pot, stir and cook until brown. Then stir-in refried beans. Add chopped onions, taco seasoning and salsa. Cook for about 10 minutes. Sprinkle the tortillas lightly with water and warm in microwave for 10 seconds. Place one tortilla on a cookie sheet and put rice in center of tortilla. Place beef mixture on top of rice and then put plenty of cheese on top of beef. Fold ends up about 2 inches. Then fold in the two sides to make a tortilla wrap. Repeat this for other tortillas. Spread salsa and shredded cheese on the top of the enchiladas and bake uncovered in 350-degree oven for 10 minutes.

CHOCOLATE CUPCAKES WITH PEANUT BUTTER FILLING

Serves 8 plus extras

Ingredients

1½ cups creamy peanut butter
2 boxes of your favorite chocolate
   cupcake mix (bake according to
   directions on box)
1 can prepared chocolate frosting

Fit a pastry bag with a small star tip. Spoon the peanut butter into the bag. Press the tip into the center of a cupcake top; squeeze the bag for 3 seconds to fill the cupcake with about ¾ tablespoon peanut butter. Be careful not to squeeze too much or you will break your cupcake apart. Using a spatula, spread icing on top of each. Add a decoration on the top by squeezing a bit of peanut butter through the star tip.

SUPER BOWL SUNDAY

The championship game is finally here. Who is going to win??

- Décor: Use team colors for your napkins and coasters,* fill plastic helmet with tortilla chips
- Table: Wheatgrass centerpiece,* place all food within reach of guests
- Activities: During commercial breaks ask five questions from sports themed Trivia Pursuit
- Favors: Little foam footballs for kids and adults!*

*Foam footballs can be found at a sports store.
*Napkins and coasters can be ordered at foryourparty.com
*Wheatgrass centerpiece at wheatgrasskits.com or profootballparties.com

Creating the Menu

Beer & Root Beer

Guacamole

Tortilla Chips & Salsa

Seven-Layer Dip

Nuts

Sweet & Sour Drumsticks

Texas Style Chili

Brownies*

*Found in the bakery section of grocery store

GUACAMOLE
Serves 8

Ingredients

⅓ cup onion, finely diced
5 tablespoons lime juice
4 avocados, halved and pitted
1 tablespoon minced seeded
   jalapeño pepper
salt and pepper, to taste

Place diced onion and minced jalapeño pepper in a medium bowl. Cut avocado in half, and spoon into onion and pepper mixture. Add lime juice, and mash with fork until smooth. Add salt and pepper.

SEVEN-LAYER DIP
Serves 8

Ingredients

1 pound ground beef
1 (8 ounce) can refried beans
2 cups shredded Cheddar-Monterey
Jack cheese blend
½ (4 ounce) sour cream
½ cup guacamole
½ cup salsa
1 (2.25 ounce) can black olives,
  chopped
¼ cup chopped tomatoes
¼ cup chopped green onions

In a large skillet, brown ground beef. Set aside to drain and cool to room temperature. Spread the beans in the bottom of a 9x13 inch serving dish that is about 1½ inches deep. Sprinkle 1 cup of shredded cheese on top of beans. Sprinkle beef on top of cheese. Spread sour cream carefully on top of beef. Spread guacamole on top of sour cream. Pour salsa over guacamole and spread evenly. Sprinkle remaining shredded cheese. Sprinkle black olives, tomatoes, and chopped green onions on top. You can serve this dish immediately, or refrigerate it overnight and serve cold.

SWEET & SOUR CHICKEN DRUMSTICKS

Serves 10

Ingredients

1 cup balsamic vinegar
1 cup honey
1 cup light brown sugar, packed
½ cup soy sauce
10 fresh rosemary sprigs
8 garlic cloves, halved
24 to 26 chicken drumsticks
4 tablespoons toasted sesame seeds
½ cup chopped fresh flat-leaf
   parsley leaves

Combine the balsamic vinegar, honey, brown sugar, soy sauce, rosemary sprigs, and garlic cloves in a large, resealable plastic bag. Shake and squeeze the contents of the bag to dissolve the honey and the brown sugar. Add the chicken drumsticks to the bag and seal, squeezing out as much air from the bag as possible. Marinate in the refrigerator for 2 hours. Preheat the oven to 450 degrees F. Line a rimmed baking sheet with aluminum foil. Remove the chicken drumsticks from the bag, reserving the marinade, and arrange them on the prepared baking sheet. Bake until the skin is caramelized and very dark in spots, 30 to 35 minutes.

Meanwhile, place the marinade in a small saucepan. Bring to a boil, then reduce the heat to a simmer and cook over low heat until thick, about 15 minutes.

Use a pastry brush to brush some of the cooked marinade on the cooked chicken. Place the chicken on a serving platter. Sprinkle with the sesame seeds and the chopped parsley.

TEXAS STYLE CHILI
Serves 8

Ingredients

1 yellow onion, finely chopped
1 teaspoon garlic, minced
2 tablespoons olive oil or vegetable oil

4 pounds chuck tender, or other beef cut suitable for chili, remove the fat and gristle, diced in small (½˝) cubes

Special Note: It is essential that you use only fresh new spices. Same goes for the garlic and onion-Fresh is best!

First Spice Blend
¼ teaspoon each cayenne pepper
   and salt
3 teaspoons chili powder
1 teaspoon ground cumin

Second Spice Blend
½ cup chili powder
4 teaspoons each cumin and paprika
¼ teaspoon cinnamon
½ teaspoon each ground oregano
   and cayenne pepper

Sauté the onion and garlic in the oil until they are transparent or soft. Add the chili meat and sprinkle the First Spice Blend over it. Mix well and cover. Cook covered until all the "red" is gone out of the meat and it is bubbling in juices. Add the following:
Two 8 ounce cans tomato sauce
2 14½-ounce cans beef stock/broth.
Cook one hour. At the end of the first hour add one-half of the Second Spice Blend mixture.

Salt lightly, you can always add more at the end if needed. Cook one more hour at a simmer, covered. Stir often and add a little water, as needed. Allow the "gravy" to start cooking down, no more than ½ inch above the meat.

At the end of the second hour, add the remaining half of the Second Spice Blend. The gravy should now begin to thicken and get smooth and creamy. Take the lid off at this point and let it simmer uncovered. Stir often. Cook another half hour or so, until the meat is very tender, and the gravy is like a thick soup. The last hour, adjust your spices sparingly; the taste will change as the spices cook in. If you like your chili hotter, you can add more cayenne at the end of the first hour, but, once the chili gets too hot, there's not a lot you can do about it. When it is done, you can adjust the flavor with a spoonful at a time of chili powder or cumin, or both. This is also the time to adjust the salt if needed.

If you have a camping stove or a low burner on your grill, this is lots of fun to do outdoors on a crisp fall day. Serve warm with side dishes of beans (most people use Ranch-style beans) grated cheddar cheese, and chopped green or yellow onions, Yum!

LOTS OF HUGS
GO FOR IT
YOU'RE TOPS WITH ME
YOU ARE MY SUNSHINE
IT'S NOW OR NEVER
REAL LUV
SMALL TALK
BE GOOD TO ME
WILL YOU BE MINE?
PEG OF MY HEART
SWEETHEART
WILL YOU BE MINE?
I WON'T TELL YOU
KISS ME AGAIN
SWEET HEARTS
SMILE
GO FOR IT
COOL MAN
MARRY ME
WALKING IN THE RAIN
I WISH YOU WOULD
TOO MUCH
LOVE YOU
GOOD BYE
HOW NICE

VALENTINE'S DAY

OO la~la!! You'll woo your sweetheart all over again, and neither of you will ever forget this delightful dinner for two.

- Décor: Red/pink/white colors, place candles around the room and keep the lights low
- Table: Have a big bouquet of red roses in the center of the table with candy hearts scattered around
- Activities: Tell your significant other five things you love about him/her
- Music: Barry White
- Favors: Red velvet boxes of chocolates

Creating the Menu

Champagne or Favorite Bottle of Wine

Razzmatazz Dip

Ready-made Salad*

Heart Shaped Ravioli* in Cream Sauce

Roasted Fingerling Potatoes*

Sautéed Spinach*

Chocolate Hearts

Pick your favorite ready-made salad from your local grocery store.
Heart Shaped Ravioli can be ordered online at alfonsogourmetpasta.com
The Potatoes and Spinach recipes can be found at allrecipes.com.

RAZZMATAZZ DIP
Serves 8 to 10

Ingredients

1 cup mayonnaise
1 teaspoon cayenne pepper (or to taste)
1 bunch green onions
1 cup Colby cheese
1 cup cheddar cheese
2 cups chopped pecans
1 pint fresh raspberries
1 small jar raspberry preserves
1 box of table crackers

Blend mayonnaise and cayenne pepper well. Add 1½ cups of pecans and stir well. Stir in the onions. Fold cheeses into mixture; it begins to thicken at this state. Shape onto plate (if you are making this the night before then refrigerate at this stage) Soften raspberry preserves in microwave for up to one minute. Pour the sauce on top of formed cheese mold all the way to the edge and allow dripping over. Place fresh raspberries on top then sprinkle remaining pecans over the entire dish. Refrigerate until ready to serve with table crackers.

CREAM SAUCE
Serves 8

Ingredients

1 quart tomato sauce
¾ cup heavy cream, at room
  temperature
½ of medium sized onion, chopped
¼ lb prosciutto, chopped
2 tablespoons olive oil
2 teaspoons white truffle oil
1 tablespoon brown sugar
salt and pepper, to taste

Place oil in a large saucepan. Sauté onions on medium heat for about 3 minutes. Add tomato sauce, heavy cream, prosciutto, white truffle oil and brown sugar. Let it cook on medium heat for about 20 minutes. Then taste and add salt and pepper, if needed. Usually the prosciutto has enough salt in it.

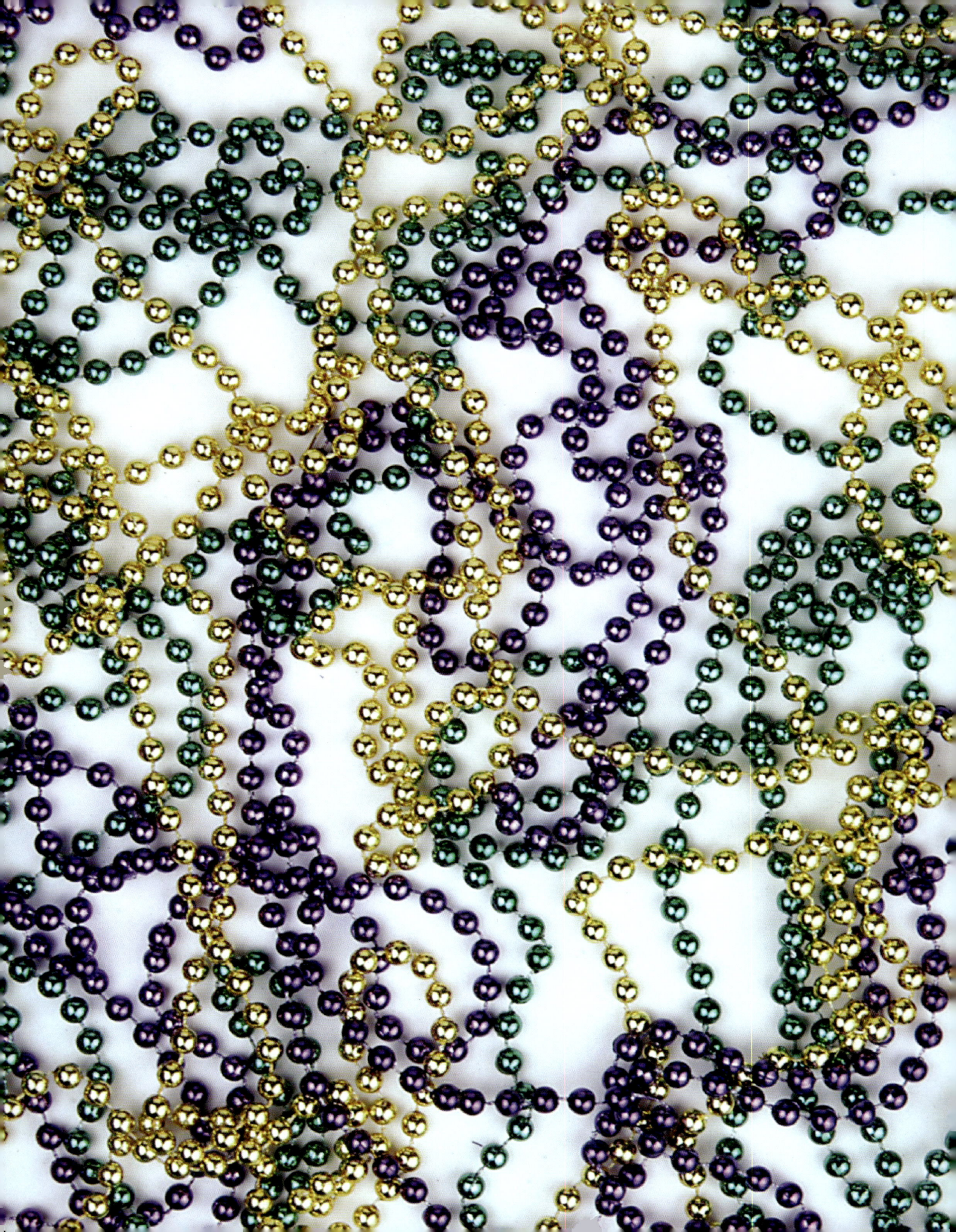

MARDI GRAS

Can we say BEADS, BEADS, and more BEADS!!

- Décor: Green/Purple/Gold Colors
- Table: Mardi Gras Beads heaped in the center, Place all the food on a side table, buffet style
- Activities: Whoever gets the little hidden prize in their piece of cake wins!
- Music: Big Chief by Professor Longhair, Street Parade by Earl King, Mardi Gras Mambo by The Hawkettes
- Favors: Bead Necklace*

*Bead necklaces can be found at any party store.

Creating the Menu

Mint Juleps & Mardi Gras Mojito*

Simple Jambalaya with Shrimp & Sausage

Cajun Spiced Shrimp & Grit cakes

Mama's Candied Yams & Merle's Spinach Balls*

King Cake*

*For Mint Juleps, Mardi Gras Mojito, and Mamas Candied Yams and Merles' Spinach Balls recipes: mardigrasday.com
*King cake is available at grocery stores

SIMPLE JAMBALAYA WITH SHRIMP & SAUSAGE
Serves 8

Ingredients

Cajun spice seasoning, to taste
4 tablespoons olive oil
2 cups diced onion
1 cup thinly sliced celery
1 cup diced carrots
2 12 ounce packages andouille
    sausage, sliced in 1 inch pieces
4 cups cooked jasmine rice*
2 14½ ounce cans diced tomatoes
    with green chilies
2 cups chicken broth
2 pounds fresh raw shrimp, peeled and
    deveined

* Cook jasmine rice according to package
  directions.

Heat oil in 4-quart pan over medium heat. Add onion, celery, and carrots. Add salt and pepper to taste. Cover and cook for 5 minutes. Add cooked rice. Then add tomatoes, broth, and shrimp. Stir and let it cook for another 5 minutes. Yumma-yumm!

CAJUN SPICED SHRIMP & GRIT CAKES
Serves 8

Ingredients

7 cups water
2 cups stone ground grits
6 cups shredded cheddar cheese
4 tablespoons butter
4 tablespoons of extra virgin olive oil
2 pounds shrimp, peeled & deveined
2 teaspoons Cajun spice seasoning
2 cups diced tomatoes
1 tablespoon salt

Bring water to a boil in a heavy-bottomed pot, add salt and reduce heat to medium. Slowly add grits and whisk until smooth and simmering. Reduce heat to low. Cover and cook for 10 minutes. Slowly whisk in cheese and 1 tablespoon of butter. Pour mixture into a loaf pan and let sit until firm.

In a large sauce pan add oil, over medium heat. Sauté shrimp for a few minutes until they begin to turn pink. Add Cajun spice and diced tomatoes.

Cut grit loaf into slices, about 1/2 inch thick. Brown slices in remaining 1 tablespoon butter in a skillet. Remove and serve each topped with shrimp and tomato sauce.

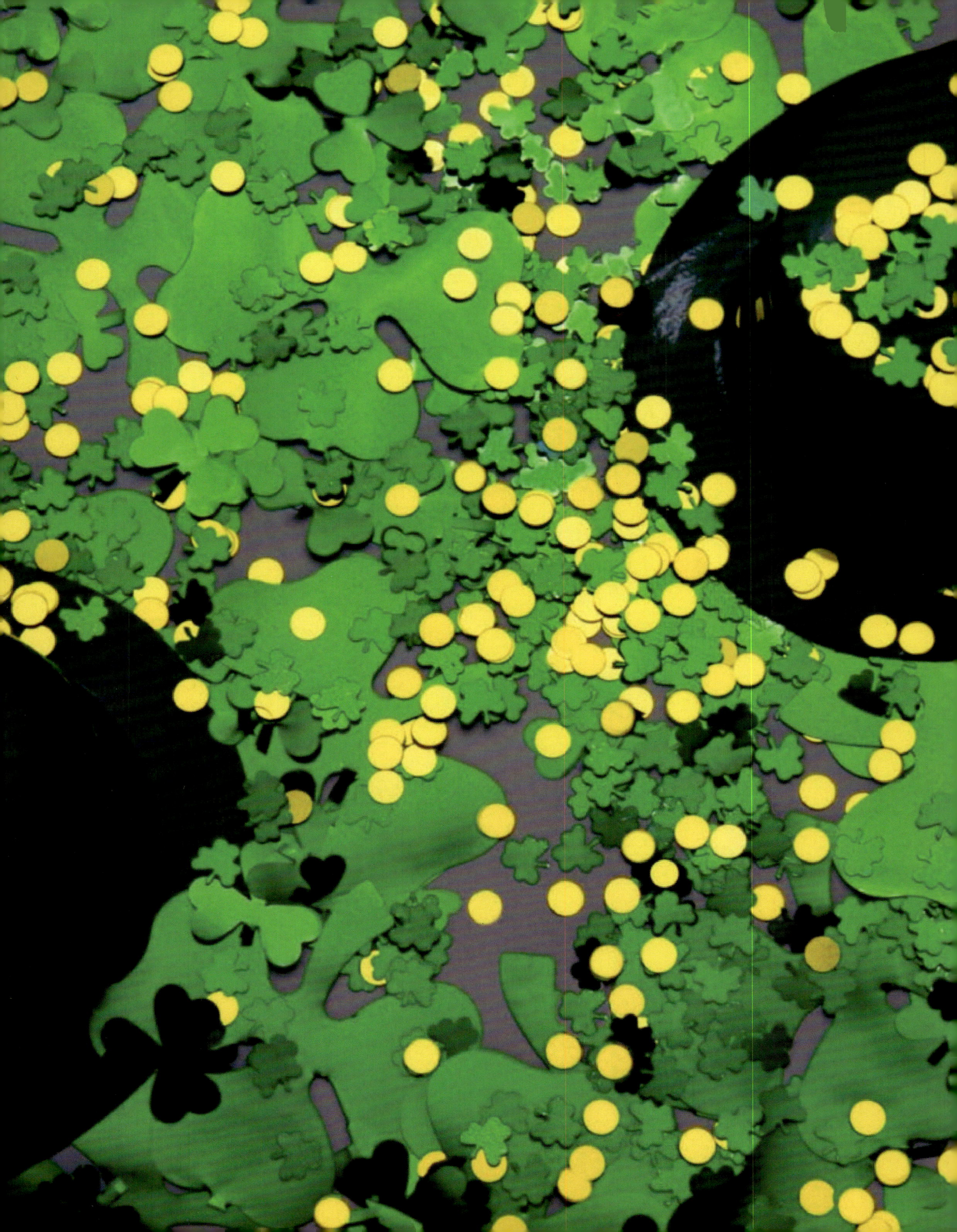

ST. PATRICK'S DAY

Think IRISH and GREEN!

- Décor: Green colors, Clovers, Hats
- Table: Green Vase and Flowers
- Favors: Foil Wrapped Chocolate Shamrock Medallions*

*Foil wrapped Chocolate Shamrock Medallions can be found at
keepsakefavors.com

Creating the Menu

Guinness Green Beer

Spinach Dip

Spinach Penne

Green Beans

Irish Soda Bread*

Irish Chocolate Mousse Cake & Irish Coffee*

*For Irish Soda Bread, Irish Chocolate Mousse Cake and Irish Coffee
find great recipes on allrecipes.com

SPINACH PENNE
Serves 8

This recipe may not be traditional Irish but it's green

Ingredients

1 pound asparagus trimmed and cut into 2-inch lengths
1 pound peas
1 avocado halved, pitted peeled and cut into ½ inch slices
1 tablespoon fresh lemon juice
1 package of spinach penne
¼ cup extra virgin olive oil
2 cloves garlic, minced
1 teaspoon salt
½ cup parsley, chopped
¼ cup shredded Parmesan cheese
4 slices pancetta (sliced and diced ¼" thick from your local deli)

Cook asparagus in a pot of boiling water, two minutes until bright green, remove. Add peas and cook 30 seconds, remove. Prepare avocado, sprinkle with lemon juice. Cook pasta per package directions. Drain and set aside. Place olive oil, asparagus, peas, garlic, pancetta, salt and pepper in the pasta cooking pot. Cook about 2 minutes. Add cooked pasta, avocado, parsley and cheese. Toss to combine, and season with additional salt and pepper if needed. Serve topped with choice of garnish and additional cheese if desired.

GREEN BEANS
Serves 8

Ingredients

1½ pounds fresh green beans
6 tablespoons butter
salt & pepper, to taste

Trim the ends off the beans and sauté in the butter in frying pan for about 10 minutes, or until crispy tender. Add salt and pepper to taste. Delicious and easy!

APRIL FOOL'S DAY

Tricks, Trix, Triiiiicks! Just wait until you spring these recipes on your guests!! They will think the main dish is dessert and you will have the last laugh.

- Décor: Yellow and White colors, poppers
- Favors: A cute practical joke gift

Creating the Menu

Gelatin Drinks

Seedless Grapes

Pita chips & Hummus

Greek-Style Salad

Meatloaf Cupcake

Peas

Grilled Pound Cake Surprise

GELATIN DRINKS
Serves 8

When your guests go to drink this they will be surprised!

Ingredients

4 boxes of 3-ounce gelatin mix
   (your favorite flavor)
8 Straws

Following the package directions to make the gelatin mix. Pour the mixture into clear glasses and insert a drinking straw into each. Place the glasses in the refrigerator to set. When they're ready, serve the jiggling juice to guests that are looking for a cool drink.

MEATLOAF CUPCAKE
Makes 12 cupcakes

Ingredients

For the Cupcake:
1 pound lean ground beef
½ cup seasoned breadcrumbs
1 cup grated Monterey Jack cheese
3 tablespoons ketchup
1 egg
½ teaspoon celery salt
½ teaspoon pepper

For the Potato Frosting:
3 cups mashed potatoes
Food coloring

Heat the oven to 375 degrees F. Line 12 muffin tin cups with foil bake cups. In a large bowl, mix together all of the meatloaf ingredients until well combined. Divide the mixture evenly among the lined cups (the liners should be about three quarters full).
Place the filled muffin tins on cookie sheets and bake the cupcakes for about 15 minutes or until cooked through. Divide the mashed potatoes among three small bowls and stir a few drops of food coloring into each batch to create blue, yellow, and pink pastel frostings. Spread a generous dollop on each little cupcake.

GREEK–STYLE SALAD

Serves 8

Dressing

Ingredients

½ cup red-wine vinegar
2 teaspoons coarse salt
1 teaspoon dried oregano
1 cup olive oil
pepper, to taste

Whisk together vinegar, salt, and oregano, and season with pepper. Add oil in a slow, steady stream and whisk.

Salad

Ingredients

24 ounces romaine hearts, leaves
  separated
1 cup pitted kalamata olives drained
1 cup pepperoncini, drained
½ cup capers, drained
4 medium tomatoes cut into
  1-inch wedges
4 cucumbers cut into 1-inch pieces
2 medium yellow onions, thinly sliced
8 ounces feta cheese, crumbled

Arrange lettuce on a platter. Scatter olives, pepperoncini, caper berries, tomatoes, cucumbers, onion, and feta over top. Drizzle with dressing.

GRILLED POUND CAKE SURPRISE

Serves 8

Ingredients

2 cups ready-made white frosting
16 drops of yellow food coloring *
8 drops of red food coloring*
16 pieces of pound cake*

* If you can find 100% natural orange food
  coloring, that is better.
* Pound cake can be found at grocery store.

Cut the pound cake into 16 bread-like slices and toast them in a toaster oven, or place under the oven broiler just until they turn golden brown. (Caution: You only need to place under broiler for a minute or two). Let cool for a few minutes. Tint the white frosting by stirring in 16 drops of yellow and 8 drops of red food coloring (to get a shade of orange that resembles American cheese).

Carefully spread and mound the frosting on one slice, then top it with the other and gently press down, the frosting will ooze out a bit and look all the more like melted cheese. Stack two slices for each sandwich and cut the stack in half diagonally.

EASTER

It's time to decorate and look for eggs!!!

- Décor: Pastel purple, yellow & pink colors, fill glass jars with layers of candy
- Activities: Dye eggs, and use stick-on decorations, have an Easter Egg Hunt, find gift baskets
- Favors: Send them home with the dyed eggs

Creating the Menu

Sodas & Juices

Fruit Platter

Spring Salad

Beef Stroganoff with Yogurt & Dill

Oven-Roasted Asparagus

Cupcakes

SPRING SALAD
Serves 8

Ingredients

¼ cup olive oil
1 teaspoon finely grated lemon zest
3 tablespoons fresh lemon juice (from 1 lemon)
1 tablespoon white-wine vinegar
1 teaspoon sugar
salt and pepper
2 heads Boston lettuce, cored & torn into bite-size pieces
1 head radicchio, cored & torn into bite-size pieces
1 pint grape tomatoes, halved

Make vinaigrette: In a small bowl, whisk together oil, lemon zest and juice, vinegar, and sugar; season with salt and pepper.

When ready to serve salad, place lettuce, radicchio, and tomatoes in a large bowl; add vinaigrette, and toss to combine. Serve immediately.

OVEN-ROASTED ASPARAGUS
Serves 8

Ingredients

2 pounds slender asparagus, trimmed
1 tablespoon extra virgin olive oil
½ teaspoon sea salt
freshly ground pepper, to taste

Preheat oven to 425 degrees F. Peel bottom half of each asparagus stalk. Toss asparagus with oil, salt, and pepper on a rimmed baking sheet. Roast until tender and golden, about 15 minutes.

BEEF STROGANOFF WITH YOGURT & DILL
Serves 8

Ingredients

24 ounces egg noodles
4 tablespoons olive oil
2 pounds sirloin steak, thinly sliced
salt and pepper, to taste
2 pounds button mushrooms, sliced
8 shallots, sliced
1 cup dry white wine
½ cup nonfat Greek yogurt
½ cup chopped fresh dill

Cook the noodles according to the package directions. Meanwhile, heat 1 tablespoon of the oil in a large skillet over medium-high heat. Season the steak with ½ teaspoon salt and pepper. In 2 batches, cook the steak until browned, about 1 minute per side, transfer to a plate.

Return the skillet to a medium heat and add the remaining tablespoon of oil. Add the mushrooms and shallots and cook, stirring occasionally, until tender 5 to 6 minutes. Add the wine and simmer until the liquid has reduced by half, 2 to 3 minutes. Return beef and any accumulated juices to the skillet and cook until heated through, 1 to 2 minutes. Serve over the noodles and top with yogurt and dill.

CUPCAKES
*Buy your favorite cake mix and bake
cupcakes according to directions*

Frosting Ingredients

1½ cups unsalted softened butter
6 cups confectioner's sugar
½ cup milk
½ teaspoon vanilla extract
Assorted pastel food colorings (blue,
    yellow, pink, green)
colored sprinkles

Beat butter, sugar, milk and vanilla
on low speed to blend, then on
high speed for 2 minutes, until good
spreading consistency. Divide frosting
into bowls and tint to desired colors.
Transfer frosting to plastic bags and
snip off one corner. Pipe in swirled
pattern on cooled cupcakes. Top off
with sprinkles.

MOTHER'S DAY

If ever there was a holiday you do not want to miss, this is THE ONE!

- Décor: Lots of flowers with love
- Activities: Make a list of 10 sweet things you will do for mom this year
- Favors: Hugs and Kisses for her

Creating the Menu

Grapefruit & Sparkling Water

Strawberry & Mozzarella Salad

Veal Cutlets with Prosciutto

Italian Peas

Dessert Crepes with Strawberries
(Strawberries are in season)

STRAWBERRY & MOZZARELLA SALAD
Serves 8

Ingredients

4 tablespoons olive oil
2 tablespoons balsamic vinegar
½ teaspoon salt
2 hearts romaine lettuce, torn into bite
   size pieces
2 8-ounce containers of strawberries,
   hulled and sliced
6 ounces mozzarella cheese, diced
½ cup fresh basil leaves

In a small bowl, mix together the oil, vinegar, salt, and pepper. Place the lettuce onto 8 salad plates. Toss the strawberries with the remaining dressing and place some of the berries on top of each lettuce plate. Top each with cheese and sprinkle with basil.

ITALIAN PEAS
Serves 8

Ingredients

3 tablespoons olive oil
2½ cloves garlic, minced
24 ounces frozen peas
2 tablespoons chicken stock
salt and pepper, to taste

Heat olive oil in a skillet over medium heat. Stir in onion and garlic. Let cook for 5 minutes. Add frozen peas and chicken stock. Add salt and pepper. Then cook for an additional 10 minutes.

VEAL CUTLETS WITH PROSCIUTTO
Serves 8

Ingredients

16 (4 ounce) veal cutlets
salt and pepper
flour for dredging
4 eggs, beaten
breadcrumbs
8 tablespoons butter
16 thin slices prosciutto
Parmigiano-Reggiano cheese, shaved
½ cup chicken stock
cherry tomatoes

Season the veal with salt and pepper and dredge each cutlet in the flour, shaking off any excess. Dip each cutlet in the beaten eggs and then into the breadcrumbs, coating them on both sides. In a large skillet over medium heat, melt the butter. Add the cutlets and cook until golden, about four minutes per side. When you flip the cutlets, top each one with a slice of prosciutto and some Parmesan shavings. Add the chicken stock and simmer until the cheese is melted. Garnish with cherry tomatoes and serve.

DESSERT CREPES WITH STRAWBERRIES
Serves 8

Ingredients

2 cups all-purpose flour
4 eggs
2 cups milk
1 cup water
½ teaspoon salt
4 tablespoons butter, melted

TOPPING
1 can whipped cream
4 cups sliced strawberries

In a large mixing bowl, whisk together the flour and the eggs. Gradually add in the milk and water and then stir. Add the salt and butter and beat until smooth. Heat a lightly oiled griddle or frying pan over medium high heat. Pour or scoop the batter onto the griddle, using approximately 1/4 cup for each crepe. Tilt the pan with a circular motion so that the batter coats the surface evenly. Cook the crepe for about 2 minutes, until the bottom is light brown. Loosen with a spatula, turn and cook the other side. Gently fold crepes in half. Then place whipped cream and cut strawberries on top of each one.

MEMORIAL DAY

In celebration and remembrance of all of those who served our country, so that we could enjoy our freedoms.

• Décor: American flags
• Table: Set the table outside using red & white checked table cloth
• Activities: A water balloon toss!

Creating the Menu

Lemonade

Mozzarella & Tomato Skewers

Chicken Piccata, Creamed Spinach

Strawberries Dipped in Whipped Cream

MOZZARELLA & TOMATO SKEWERS
Serves 8

Ingredients

40 small fresh mozzarella balls
40 cherry tomatoes
40 basil leaves
1½ tablespoons chives, finely chopped
8 tablespoons extra virgin olive oil
salt and pepper, to taste

Thread the 5 mozzarellas, 5 tomatoes, and 5 basil leaves onto each skewer in alternating order. Transfer the skewers to a serving platter and sprinkle with the chives. Season skewers with salt and pepper, drizzle with the olive oil, and serve.

CHICKEN PICCATA
Serves 8

Ingredients

8 skinless, boneless chicken cutlets
4 tablespoons of fresh lemon juice
2 teaspoons lemon zest
1 cup flour
1 teaspoon salt
1 teaspoon freshly ground black
  pepper
4 tablespoons extra virgin olive oil
½ cup capers, drained
1 cup dry white wine
1½ cups chicken broth
4 tablespoons chopped parsley

Place chicken cutlets between 2 sheets of waxed paper or plastic wrap. With a mallet, gently pound cutlets to ¼ inch thickness. Zest and juice the lemon. In a shallow bowl, combine flour, lemon zest, salt and pepper. Dip chicken in flour, coat all sides and shake off excess. Preheat a large sauté pan over medium heat. Add olive oil and tilt pan until a thin layer covers the bottom. Place chicken on the hot oil and cook 3 minutes per side, until cooked through. Remove pan from heat. Transfer chicken to a plate and keep warm. Return pan to medium heat, add capers and cook for 1 minute until slightly plumped. Add white wine and chicken broth and bring to a brisk simmer, stirring with a wooden spoon to scrape up browned bits from bottom. Cook until volume is reduced by half, 3 to 4 minutes. Remove from heat, stir in parsley and 2 tablespoons lemon juice. Serve cutlets topped with sauce and capers.

CREAMED SPINACH

Serves 8

Ingredients

1½ tablespoon olive oil
1 onion, finely chopped
1 garlic clove, chopped
¼ teaspoon each salt and black
  pepper
¾ of 8-ounce bar of cream cheese
1 cup of milk
27 ounce package frozen chopped
  spinach, thawed

Heat the oil in a large skillet over medium heat. Add the onion, garlic, ¼ teaspoon salt, and ¼ teaspoon pepper and cook, stirring, until soft, 6 to 7 minutes. Add the cream cheese and milk and cook, stirring, until the cream cheese is melted. Squeeze any excess liquid out of the spinach, add the spinach to the sauce, and cook until the mixture is heated through and thickened, 3 to 4 minutes.

STRAWBERRIES DIPPED IN WHIPPED CREAM

Serves 8

Ingredients

16 strawberries
2 cups whipped cream

Dip strawberries in the whipped cream and arrange on a platter.

FATHER'S DAY

Dad's the man; you know it, now show it with love and great food!

- Décor: Shades of blue
- Table: Place tools in a glass jar for centerpiece
- Activities: Write ten things you admire most about dad and present them on a certificate of merit

Creating the Menu

Red Wine

Caprese Bruschetta

Pasta Bolognese

Garlic Baguette*

Gelato & Biscotti*

Whole Foods has a great frozen one called Alexia Garlic Baguette. It is incredible!!

Pick up Gelato and Biscotti from Whole Foods. Many other grocery stores will have both these items as well.

CAPRESE BRUSCHETTA
Serves 8

Ingredients

1 large French baguette
1 tomato, chopped
1 large mozzarella cheese ball,
  diced
fresh basil, chopped
Balsamic Vinaigrette dressing

Toast French baguette slices. Top with chopped tomatoes, diced fresh mozzarella cheese, and chopped fresh basil. Drizzle with Balsamic Vinaigrette dressing.

PASTA BOLOGNESE
Serves 8

Ingredients

2 tablespoons olive oil
1 garlic clove, minced
1 pound lean ground sirloin
salt and pepper
1 can crushed tomatoes
1 can Progresso tomato puree
1 can traditional Ragu sauce
2 teaspoons sugar (to decrease
   acidity)
2 teaspoons oregano
2 teaspoons basil
1 pound spaghetti

Cook spaghetti pasta according to box directions. Add two tablespoons olive oil to pasta water to keep it from boiling over.

Heat 1 tablespoon of olive oil in a large pot over medium heat. Add minced garlic. Add ground sirloin and use spoon to chop it up and mix. Cook until meat is brown. Pour in crushed tomatoes, puree, and tomato sauce. Add sugar, salt and pepper. Then add oregano and basil. Then mix into pasta.

BASKETBALL FINALS

Not everyone follows every game during basketball season, but the championships are not to be missed!

- Décor: Your favorite team colors
- Table: Set up food on table buffet style
- Favors: Mini basketballs from any party store

Creating the Menu

Beer & Soda

Vegetable Platter with Dip*

Sloppy Joes

Tomato, Olive & Parmesan Pizza

Chocolate Chip Cookies*

*Find ready-made vegetable platters and dip at most local grocery stores.

*Otis Spunkmeyer chocolate chip cookie dough is a great one.
Follow recipe on package.

SLOPPY JOES
Serves 6 to 8

This is a mouthwatering meal...you'll need several napkins.

Ingredients

1 pound lean ground beef
1 medium onion, diced
4 cloves garlic, minced
1 medium red bell pepper, seeded
   and diced
1 15.5 ounce can small red or pinto
   beans, drained and rinsed
1½ cups tomato sauce
2 tablespoons tomato paste
1 tablespoon red wine vinegar
1 tablespoon unsulfured molasses
1 tablespoon Worcestershire sauce
3⁄4 teaspoon salt
8 whole-wheat burger buns

Brown the meat and onion in a large nonstick skillet over medium-heat for 5 minutes, breaking up the meat into crumbles as it cooks. Pour the drippings out of the pan and discard. Add the garlic and red pepper and cook 5 minutes more, stirring occasionally. Stir in beans, tomato sauce, tomato paste, red wine vinegar, unsulfured molasses, and Worcestershire sauce. Reduce the heat to low, and simmer for another 5 minutes. Serve on buns.

TOMATO, OLIVE & PARMESAN PIZZA
Serves 8

Ingredients

8 6-in. diameter whole-wheat tortillas
4 medium ripe tomatoes, seeded and
  chopped
1 cup pitted and coarsely chopped
kalamata olives or black olives
4 teaspoons olive oil
½ cup freshly grated Parmesan
  cheese
4 tablespoons torn fresh basil leaves
ground pepper, to taste

Preheat oven to 400 degrees F. Put the tortillas on a baking sheet and top each with the tomatoes and olives. Drizzle with the olive oil, add cheese, and bake until crisp and the cheese is slightly melted, about 10 minutes. Garnish with basil and season with pepper. Let cool for a few minutes, then slice each into 4 wedges and serve.

FOURTH OF JULY

July 4th, 1776 is a date that will be remembered forever. It is a proud day to celebrate Liberty and Opportunity.

- Décor: A container of red, white, and blue flags, red, white, and blue flowers
- Table: Sparklers, and red, white, and blue sand candles
- Activities: Fireworks, perhaps see a parade, have a balloon toss and tug of war
- Music: *The Star-Spangled Banner, God Bless America, Stars and Stripes Forever* and *Firework* by Katy Perry
- Favors: Flags

Creating the Menu

Sparkling Raspberry Lemonade

Sparkling Pomegranate Blueberry Lemonade*

Tequila soaked watermelon wedges

Tomato Brie Pasta

Hot Dogs & Hamburgers

Vanilla ice cream with Raspberries & Blueberries on top

* Lemonade can be found at most grocery stores

SPARKLING RASPBERRY LEMONADE
Serves 8

Ingredients

5 cups sparkling water
2 cups lemonade
3 cups raspberry juice (or cranberry
  raspberry juice)
2 cups ice
1 cup of raspberries

In a large pitcher, add ice, sparkling water, lemonade, and raspberry juice. Mix all together with a large spoon. Then place raspberries on top.

TEQUILA-SOAKED WATERMELON WEDGES
Serves 8

Ingredients

1 seedless watermelon, cut into 1 inch
  thick wedges
1 cup sugar
¾ cup water
½ cup tequila
¼ cup triple sec
2 limes, halved
sea salt

Arrange watermelon in a single layer in two 9-by-13-inch baking dishes. Bring sugar, water, tequila, and triple sec to a boil in a small saucepan. Cook, stirring, until sugar dissolves, about 1 minute. Let cool slightly. Pour syrup over watermelon wedges, and refrigerate 45 minutes. Remove watermelon from syrup and arrange on a platter. Squeeze limes over and season with sea salt.

TOMATO BRIE PASTA
Serves 8

Ingredients

4 ripe tomatoes, diced
1 pound Brie, rind removed, cut into
   irregular pieces
1 cup fresh basil, cut into strips
3 cloves of garlic, finely minced
1½ pounds linguini
1 cup olive oil
½ teaspoon pepper
2½ teaspoons salt
grated Parmesan cheese

In a large bowl, combine tomatoes, Brie, basil, garlic, olive oil, salt, and pepper. Let combination sit for two hours.

Cook linguini according to package directions. Then add hot linguini to the large bowl. Sprinkle the Parmesan on top. Serve at room temperature.

VANILLA ICE CREAM WITH RASPBERRIES & BLUEBERRIES
Serves 8

Ingredients

2 quarts of vanilla ice cream
16 ounces of blueberries
16 ounces of raspberries

In a small bowl, add 2 scoops of vanilla ice cream. Place a few blueberries on top. Then add a few raspberries on top. Repeat this for the 7 other bowls.

SUMMER BARBEQUE

Pick a nice day in August to have your own special holiday BBQ.

- Décor: Toy beach pails half full of sand, fill buckets with a bottle of tanning oil, a water spritzer and bubbles, place beach balls around the area
- Activities: Take a ride on and old fashioned slip and slide, have a bubble blowing or pie throwing contest

Creating the Menu

Tropical Lemonade & Peach Nectar Iced Tea

Potato Chips & Cheese Puffs

Barbecued Chicken

Corn on the Cob

Peach Cobbler with Vanilla Ice Cream*

*Find peach cobbler in local grocery store

TROPICAL LEMONADE
Serves 8

Ingredients

7 cups water
5 cups lemonade
2 cups ice
1 peach, sliced
2 small slices of an orange
2 small slices of a lemon
2 small slices of a lime

In a large pitcher, add ice, water, lemonade, sugar, and mix together. Then slice up one peach and place in pitcher. Slice 2 small pieces of orange, lemon, and lime and place in pitcher. Mix with a spoon and it is ready!

PEACH NECTAR ICED TEA
Serves 8-10

Ingredients

7 cups cold water
7 tea bags black tea
7 cups peach nectar
4 peaches peeled, pitted, and sliced
   into eighths

Bring the water to a boil in a saucepan. Remove from the heat. Add the tea bags, cover and let sit for 5 minutes. Remove the tea bags. Let tea cool to room temperature. Stir in the peach nectar. Serve in ice filled glasses with 2 slices of peach.

CORN ON THE COB
Serves 8

Ingredients

8 ears of corn
8 tablespoons butter, softened
salt and pepper, to taste

Pre-heat grill to high heat and lightly oil grate. Peel back corn husks and remove silk. Place 1 tablespoon of butter on each piece of corn. Close husks. Wrap each ear of corn tightly in aluminum foil. Place on the prepared grill. Cook about 30 minutes, turning occasionally, until corn is tender.

BARBECUED CHICKEN
Serves 8

Ingredients

8 pieces of chicken legs or breasts
1 cup your favorite barbeque sauce

Place chicken and sauce in a large resealable plastic bag. Turn the bag several times so the chicken is well coated. Refrigerate for 4 hours, turning the bag occasionally to distribute sauce. Remove chicken and arrange on a lightly greased, preheated grill over low coals. Cook turning frequently, until the meat near the bone is no longer pink, 30 to 45 minutes. Transfer to a platter and serve.

LABOR DAY

This is a day for fun and relaxation to give us a break from the hard work in our lives. Labor Day also marks the beginning of the football season.

• Décor: White/Ivory/Blue Colors
• Activity: Swim and relax by the pool

Creating the Menu

Sparkling Water, Green Tea & Beer

Refreshing Salad

Orecchiette with Mini Chicken Meatballs

Berry Trifle

Cupcakes for the Kids

REFRESHING SALAD
Serves 8

Ingredients

2 heads of romaine lettuce, julienned
1½ heads of radicchio, chopped
6 red tomatoes, diced
6 yellow tomatoes, diced
2 cucumbers, thinly sliced

Vinaigrette

4 tablespoons vinegar
4 tablespoons extra virgin olive oil
salt and pepper, to taste

In a small bowl, whisk together the vinegar and olive oil, season with salt and pepper, and set aside.

Place the romaine, radicchio, tomatoes, and cucumbers in a large serving bowl. Let guests dress their own salad.

ORECCHIETTE WITH MINI CHICKEN MEATBALLS
Serves 8 to 10

Ingredients

2 pounds orecchiette pasta
½ cup plain breadcrumbs
½ cup chopped fresh flat-leaf parsley
4 large eggs, lightly beaten
2 tablespoons whole milk
2 tablespoons ketchup
1½ cup freshly grated Romano cheese
1½ teaspoons salt
1½ teaspoons pepper
2 pounds ground chicken
½ cup olive oil
3 cups chicken broth
8 cups cherry tomatoes, halved
2 cups freshly grated Parmesan cheese
16 ounces small mozzarella balls, halved
1½ cups chopped fresh basil leaves

Bring a large pot of salted water to a boil over high-heat. Add the pasta and cook until tender but firm, 8 to 10 minutes. Drain the pasta, reserving a scant 1 cup of the pasta water. Transfer the pasta to a large serving bowl and add ½ cup of the Parmesan. Toss to coat the orecchiette lightly, adding the reserved pasta water to help make a sauce.

In a medium bowl, stir together the bread crumbs parsley, eggs, milk, ketchup, Romano cheese, salt, and pepper. Add the chicken and combine well. Using a melon baller to scoop up the mixture, roll the seasoned chicken into ¾ inch mini meatballs. Heat the oil in a large skillet over medium-high heat. Working into batches, add the meatballs and cook without moving until brown on the bottom, about two minutes. Turn the meatballs and brown the tops, about two more minutes. Add the chicken broth and tomatoes and bring to a boil, using the wooden spoon to scrape up the brown bits that cling to the bottom of the pan. Reduce the heat to low and simmer until the tomatoes are soft and the meatballs are cooked through, about 5 minutes.

Add the meatball mixture, mozzarella, and ½ cup of basil to the pasta and mix well. Garnish with the remaining Parmesan and basil.

BERRY TRIFLE

Serves 8

Ingredients

8 ounces of vanilla pudding
1 1/2 cups of whipped cream
1 (9 inch) prepared angel food cake,
  cut into 1 inch square pieces
4 cups of blueberries
2 cups of raspberries
2 cups of blackberries

Place vanilla pudding in a medium size bowl. Fold whipped cream into vanilla pudding. In a 2 quart glass serving bowl, place pieces of angel food cake on the bottom. Have the 1 inch pieces cover the bottom. With a spoon, take vanilla pudding mixture and place a layer on top of angel food cake. Place a layer of blueberries, raspberries, and blackberries. Repeat layers until berry layer is at the top. The amount of layers will depend on the type of serving bowl. Place bowl in refrigerator for about two hours.

HALLOWEEN

Trick or Treat!!

- Décor: Black/Orange/White colors, use leaves, pumpkins, ghosts, hats, black cats, candy corn, webs, and bats, carve a pumpkin with kids and decorate Trick or Treat Bags
- Table: Place pumpkins on table
- Activities: Costume Contest... Check out your guests creative costumes, place three plastic pumpkins on a table labeled—Silliest Costume, Scariest Costume, and Best Costume, have guests drop their votes in each pumpkin, tally results and reveal the winners!!
- Favors: Candy, of course!

Creating the Menu

Purple Potion Punch

Orange Soda with Black Licorice

Prosciutto Mozzarella Pinwheels

Cheesy Baked Shells and Broccoli

Orange Cupcakes & Pumpkin Trifle

ORANGE SODA WITH BLACK LICORICE

Serves 8

Ingredients

8 cups of orange soda (such as Jones
    orange soda)
8 long pieces of black licorice

Fill 8 glasses with orange soda. Place a black licorice "straw" in each glass.

PURPLE POTION PUNCH

Serves 8
(About two cups/person)

Ingredients

8 cups purple grape juice
2 cups vanilla ice cream
2 liters lemon-lime soda
confetti sprinkles

In a large pitcher, mix grape juice and melted ice cream until blended. Right before serving add soda and stir just until blended.

Pour into glasses and top each with a scoop of ice cream and sprinkles.

CHEESE BAKED SHELLS & BROCCOLI

Serves 8

Ingredients

1½ pounds pasta shells
2 tablespoons of butter
4 tablespoons all-purpose flour
4 cups whole milk
4 cups coarsely grated cheddar
  cheese
2 16-ounce bags frozen broccoli florets,
  thawed
¼ teaspoon ground nutmeg
salt and pepper, to taste

Heat broiler. Cook the pasta according to the package directions. Drain and set aside.

Meanwhile, heat the butter in a large pot over medium heat. Add the flour and cook, stirring, for two minutes. Whisk in the milk and cook, stirring occasionally, until slightly thickened, 4 to 5 minutes. Add 1½ cups of the cheese and stir until melted. Stir in the nutmeg, ¾ teaspoon salt, and ¼ teaspoon pepper. Add the pasta and broccoli and toss to combine. Transfer to a broiler proof 8-inch square or another 1¼ quart-baking dish. Sprinkle with the remaining ½ cup of cheese. Broil until golden, 3 to 4 minutes.

PROSCIUTTO MOZZARELLA PINWHEELS
Serves 8

Ingredients

Flour for dusting
1¼ pounds purchased pizza dough
2¼ cups shredded mozzarella cheese
7½ ounces prosciutto, thinly sliced
1¼ cups coarsely chopped baby
   spinach
1½ tablespoons olive oil
salt and pepper, to taste

Preheat oven to 425 degrees F. Line a baking sheet with parchment paper. On a lightly floured work surface, roll out the pizza dough into a 12-to-14-inch circle, about ¼ inch thick.

Sprinkle half of the mozzarella over the dough. Arrange the prosciutto over the cheese in a single layer. Sprinkle with the chopped spinach, and then top with the remaining cheese. Roll the dough into a thin cylinder, gently tucking in the ends. Brush the entire roll with the olive oil and season with the salt and pepper. Place the dough, seam side down, on the baking sheet. Place baking sheet in lower third of the oven and bake for 25 minutes, or until the top is golden brown. Cool the roll for 3 to 4 minutes, and then use a knife to cut it into ¾ inch wide slices. *Mmmmm!*

ORANGE CUPCAKES

Makes about 12 cupcakes
These cupcakes taste like orange cream popsicles...delicious!

Ingredients

1 box of vanilla cake mix
  (+ ingredients on the box)
1 box vanilla icing mix (+ the
  ingredients on the box)
1 tablespoon orange flavor*
1 tablespoon orange food coloring*

* Orange flavor and food coloring can be
found at any grocery store

Follow directions on box of vanilla cake mix to make cupcakes.

Follow directions on box of vanilla icing mix. Once the icing is made, add 1 tablespoon of orange food color, mix. Repeat until you have desired orange color. Then add 1 tablespoon of orange flavoring, mix. Let cupcakes cool and spread icing on top of cupcakes.

PUMPKIN TRIFLE

Serves 8

Ingredients

½ pint heavy cream
½ cup sugar
1 loaf pumpkin bread, cut into ½ inch
   thick slices
1 cup caramel sauce
2 cups prepared vanilla pudding
½ cup finely chopped pecans

In a medium bowl, using an electric mixer on medium speed, whip the cream with the sugar until stiff. Arrange the remaining ingredients except for the nuts in layers in your chosen serving dish; start with whipped cream, add some pumpkin bread, drizzle with caramel sauce, spoon on some vanilla pudding. Repeat this sequence, ending with whipped cream, until all ingredients are used. Top with nuts. Refrigerate until chilled.

THANKSGIVING

Thanksgiving is a time to be grateful for family, friends, and food. Let's celebrate this day by preparing a great traditional meal. The stuffing, green beans, cranberry sauce, and the pumpkin pie can be prepared a day in advance. The sweet potatoes, mashed potatoes, turkey and gravy can all be prepared Thanksgiving morning.

- Table: Roll up individual menus and tie with a string, place a name tag at end of string, then place inside a decorative bottle at each place setting
- Activities: Thankful quotes in a bowl to pass around

Creating the Menu

Juice & Teas

Turkey & Dressing

Sweet Potato Casserole

Mashed Potatoes

Green Bean Casserole

Cranberry Sauce

Pumpkin & Apple Pies*

Pick up a ready-made apple pie at the grocery store.

TURKEY & DRESSING
Serves 10

1 10 to 12 pound Butterball turkey

Follow directions on the package to thaw and prepare for roasting. Prepare stuffing just before you are ready to pop the turkey in the oven.

CRANBERRY & PECAN STUFFING

Ingredients

1 14-ounce package of Pepperidge
  Farm Herb Seasoned Stuffing
3 tablespoons melted butter
1 cup finely chopped yellow onion
1 cup finely chopped celery
2½ cups no fat chicken stock
1 cup dried cranberries
½ cup chopped pecans

Melt the butter in a saucepan, and sauté the chopped onion and celery until it is soft, but not browned. Place the stuffing mixture in a large bowl and mix onion and celery in, stirring it well, add the cranberries, pecans and the chicken stock. Toss well. Stuff the prepared turkey and put the remainder of the dressing in a lightly greased casserole. Cover with foil and bake at 350 degrees F for about ½ hour. Wait until the turkey is almost done before putting the casserole in the oven, because the turkey has to "rest" for about 20 minutes after it comes out of the oven.

SWEET POTATO CASSEROLE
Serves 8

Ingredients

6 medium size sweet potatoes
$1/2$ cup sugar
2 eggs
1 teaspoon vanilla extract
$1/3$ cup milk
$1/2$ cup butter
1 teaspoon cinnamon

Topping
2 tablespoons butter
$1/3$ cup firmly packed brown sugar
2 tablespoons flour
$1/2$ cup finely chopped pecans
1 teaspoon cinnamon

Preheat oven to 350 degrees F. Place sweet potatoes in oven for one hour, or until tender. Let cool, peel and mash. In large bowl, combine sweet potatoes, sugar, eggs, vanilla, milk, cinnamon, and butter. Beat, at medium speed, with an electric mixer until almost smooth. Spoon into a lightly greased 12″ x 8″ x 2″ baking dish.

For the topping:
In a large bowl, combine brown sugar, pecans, flour, cinnamon and butter. Sprinkle mixture over casserole. Bake at 350 degrees F for 30 minutes.

CRANBERRY SAUCE
Serves 8

Ingredients

1 15-ounce can whole cranberry
1 15-ounce can cranberry jelly
1 15-ounce can crushed pineapple, strained
1 15-ounce can mandarin oranges, strained
1 cup tiny marshmallows
½ cup walnuts

In a large bowl, mix whole cranberries, cranberry jelly, crushed pineapples, and mandarin oranges. Then pour ingredients from bowl into a serving bowl. Place marshmallows and walnuts on top.

PUMPKIN PIE
Serves 8

Ingredients

1 15-ounce can pumpkin puree
½ teaspoon salt
3 teaspoons pumpkin pie spice
2 eggs
¼ cup of apple butter or pumpkin
   butter
1 can sweetened evaporated milk
1 unbaked 9" deep-dish pie shell
16 scoops of vanilla ice cream

Mix pumpkin, salt, spice, eggs, and butter together in a small bowl. Then gradually stir in evaporated milk and pour into pie shell. Bake in preheated 425 degree F oven for 15 minutes. Reduce temperature to 350 degrees F for 40 minutes. Cool for 2 hours.

When ready to serve, place 2 scoops of ice cream on each dish.

CHRISTMAS

Each family has so many great Christmas Traditions and it is so nice to keep them going.

- Décor: Green/Red/White, place ball ornaments in bowls, red and white poinsettias
- Activities: Christmas gift exchange game
- Favors: White boxes with red ribbons filled with cinnamon bread
- Music: Christmas tunes

Creating the Menu

Pink Cocktail

Shrimp Cocktail & Cheese Platter

Roasted Red Peppers

Crostinis with Grapes Platter

Melon with Prosciutto

Salad

Beef Lasagna & Ham*

Dried Cherry Popover & Raspberry Trifle

Cinnamon Bread & Hot Cocoa

Beef lasagna and ham recipes can be found at www.allrecipes.com.

PINK COCKTAIL
Serves 8

Ingredients

7 ounces vodka
9 ounces pink grapefruit juice
ice cubes

Fill a large pitcher ½ full with ice cubes. Pour in vodka and then pink grapefruit juice. Stir and serve over ice.

ROASTED RED PEPPERS
Serves 8

Ingredients

4 garlic cloves, sliced
1 teaspoon parsley, chopped
1 teaspoon oregano, chopped
1/3 teaspoon salt
1/3 cup olive oil
1 12-ounce jar of roasted red peppers
crackers

Drain the jar of roasted peppers and slice thinly. Add olive oil, enough to cover the peppers. Add the parsley, sliced garlic, oregano, salt and that is it! You can always add more to this, such as fresh basil or hearts of palm. Serve with crackers

MELON WITH PROSCIUTTO
Serves 8

Ingredients

1 pound prosciutto thinly sliced
1 large cantaloupe

Cut the cantaloupe in half and remove the seeds. Using a knife, cut the rest of the cantaloupe into rather thin slices. Wrap the prosciutto around the cantaloupe and serve chilled.

DRIED CHERRY POPOVER

Serves 7

Ingredients

1 tablespoon unsalted butter, melted
3 large eggs, beaten
⅓ cup granulated sugar
¾ cup all-purpose flour
1¼ cups whole milk
½ cup dried cherries

Heat oven to 375 degrees F. Butter the bottom and sides of a 2-quart baking dish. In a bowl, combine the eggs and ⅓ cup of sugar. Whisk the flour until no lumps remain. Whisk in the milk and melted butter. Pour the batter into the prepared pan and scatter the cherries over the top. Sprinkle with the remaining sugar and bake until puffed and golden, about 45 minutes. Serve warm.

RASPBERRY TRIFLE
Serves 8

Ingredients

1 (9 in) sponge cake, cut in cubes
1 cup seedless raspberry jam
8 ounces of fresh raspberries
2½ cups heavy cream
3 egg yolks
3 tablespoons white sugar
2 ounces sliced almonds

Spread jam on each piece of cake and place in the bottom of a large glass bowl. Sprinkle raspberries over cake.

Heat 1¼ cups of cream in a medium saucepan over medium heat. While the cream is heating, beat the egg yolks with the sugar until pale yellow and smooth. Strain yolk mixture into a clean bowl. Pour hot cream into egg yolks and stir vigorously. Return mixture to the pan over low heat and cook, stirring, until thick enough to coat the back of a metal spoon. Remove from heat and allow to cool.

While custard is cooling, whip 1¼ cups of cream until soft peaks form. Place almonds on a baking sheet. Bake in 300 degree F oven until golden (usually will take 5 minutes). Spread cooled custard over cake in bowl. Top with whipped cream and toasted almonds. Chill in fridge for 2 hours, before serving.

CINNAMON BREAD

Serves 8

This is for the favors... it'll be great for the morning.

Ingredients

2 1-pound packages refrigerated pizza dough
1 tablespoon cinnamon
1 cup sugar
8 tablespoons butter, melted

Heat over to 375 degrees F. Tear off bits of dough and roll them into 1-inch balls. Place the balls on a plate. Combine the cinnamon and sugar in a bowl. Dip each ball in the butter, then the cinnamon sugar. Transfer the balls to a buttered Bundt pan. Drizzle any remaining butter over the top and sprinkle with remaining cinnamon sugar. Bake until golden brown, about 40 minutes. Remove from the oven and let cool for 5 minutes. Place on top of the pan and carefully flip it over. Tap the bottom to release the bread.

NEW YEAR'S EVE

"Should auld acquaintance be forgot, And never brought to mind?
Should auld acquaintance be forgot and auld lang syne?" Perfect, so
don't forget the fireworks, hats and horns!!!

- Décor: Silver/Black or Gold/Black
- Activities: Horns, watch fireworks, tell your New Year resolutions
- Favors: Hershey kisses in a jar

Creating the Menu

Champagne

Sugar Nut Glazed Brie

Rosemary Cashews

Chicken Spinach Pasta

Chocolate Covered Strawberries

ROSEMARY CASHEWS

Serves 8

Ingredients

1½ pounds raw whole unsalted
  cashews
2 tablespoons rosemary
½ teaspoon cayenne pepper
4 tablespoons light brown sugar
1 tablespoon salt
2 tablespoons unsalted butter, melted

Place raw cashews in an oven safe dish and bake at 350 degrees F for 4 minutes. In a medium size bowl, mix together the rosemary, cayenne pepper, light brown sugar, Kosher salt, and unsalted butter. Add the cashews and stir well to mix.

SUGAR NUT GLAZED BRIE
Serves 8

Ingredients

¼ cup packed light brown sugar
¼ cup chopped pecans or walnuts
1 tablespoon brandy
1 14-ounce wheel of Brie, peel and
   take off the white covering on top of
   Brie
Serve with crackers, apple wedges,
   grapes

Preheat oven to 500 degrees F. In a jar, stir together sugar, nuts and brandy. Place cheese on a large ovenproof platter. Bake for 5 minutes. Sprinkle sugar on top of cheese and bake until sugar is melted and cheese is heated through. Serve with fruits and crackers.

CHICKEN SPINACH PASTA
Serves 8

Ingredients

1 pound pasta (preferably penne)
1 box leaf spinach
1 can sun-dried tomatoes
½ cup pine nuts
½ cup mushrooms
4 boneless, skinless chicken breasts
2 tablespoons olive oil
½ cup onions, sliced
½ cup fresh tomato, diced

Cook pasta according to directions. Penne pasta goes great with this dish. In a separate large skillet, medium heat, start sautéing chicken in the oil. Once chicken is cooked, take out and cut into 1 inch slices. In the large skillet, add onions, stir for a few minutes and then add mushrooms. Let it cook for two more minutes. Next add in tomato, spinach, and sun-dried tomatoes. Add it all to the pasta and mix together well. Then add chicken to pasta and mix. Sprinkle pine nuts on top.

ACKNOWLEDGEMENTS & CREDITS

I would especially like to thank my family and friends for inspiring me to create this book. I also would like to thank the following for their wonderful recipes and help...

Holly Galesi
Ginnie Siena Bivona
Michael Castellano
M. Mark Castellano II
Biz Haddock
Laura Pennington
Joan Soilleux
Jane Castellano
Rita Lloyd
Camilla Solari
Tina Burns
Ocean Castle, LLC
Cottage Living Magazine
Natural Home Magazine
Familyfun.com
Family Circle
Italian Cooking and Living Magazine
Allrecipes.com
Wholefoods.com
Martha Stewart Magazine
Marthastewart.com
Silver Palate Cookbook
Giada's Cooking
Giada's Kitchen
Woman's Day Magazine
Real Simple Magazine
Entertaining Simple

INDEX

To Order Additional Copies of this Book:

www.mcreationsllc.com

Or

www.amazon.com

A GREAT GIFT FOR HOLIDAYS & BIRTHDAYS